Frog

Huggums

Bun Bun

Little Sister

Gator

Bat Child

Maurice & Molly

Oscar

Bun Bun's Birthday

by MERCER MAYER

Bun Bun's Birthday

by MERCER MAYER

It was Bun Bun's birthday. But no one wished her a happy birthday. And there were no birthday cards in the mailbox. Maybe everyone just forgot, Bun Bun thought.

"Did you forget anything today,
Little Critter?" Bun Bun asked.
"I forgot to put icing on this
carrot cake," Little Critter said.

"Did you forget anything, Seaweed?"
Bun Bun asked. "I forgot to put sugar
in this lemonade," Seaweed said.

"Did you forget anything today?" Bun Bun asked
Maurice and Molly.
"We forgot to buy candles," Maurice and Molly said.
"We just ran to the store to get them."

"Did you forget anything, Skat Owl?" Bun Bun asked.

"I forgot that I must be somewhere special soon," said Skat Owl.

"Did you forget anything, Bat Child?"
Bun Bun asked.
"Yes," said Bat Child. "I forgot
to practice a special song
on my guitar."

"Did you forget anything,
Possum Child?"
Bun Bun asked.

"No," said Possum Child. "All I had to do
was wrap something, and I did it."

"Did you forget anything, Frog and Mouse?" Bun Bun asked.
"No," Frog and Mouse said.

"We just had to blow up some balloons."

Bun Bun walked home sadly.

Everyone forgot my birthday, Bun Bun thought.
She went into her house and closed her door.

Bun Bun put on an old party hat.
She stuck a candle in a piece of moldy old bread
and began to sing "Happy Birthday."
Suddenly, there was a knock on the door.